# 5 Minute
# BEDTIME
## TALES

# Time For Bed!

Choose your sleepytime story by looking at the index
at the back.

# 5 Minute
# BEDTIME
## TALES

WRITTEN BY NICOLA BAXTER
ILLUSTRATED BY JENNY PRESS

ARMADILLO

This edition published in 2002
by Armadillo Books
an imprint of
Bookmart Limited
Registered Number 2372865
Desford Road
Enderby
Leicester
LE9 5AD

© 1999 Bookmart Limited

ISBN 1-84322-113-6

Printed in Slovakia

# Contents

# Fred-Under-the-Bed

When the children's mother saw that Jake and Rosie were still playing, she told them to go to bed at once.

"But there's a Fred under Jake's bed!" cried the twins.

"What *do* you mean?" asked their mother. "There's nothing under your beds except odd socks and probably more dust than there should be."

"But it's what happens to socks," said Jake. "They turn into sock monsters. Ours is called Fred."

"That's enough," said his mother. "Get into bed right now. I'm putting the light out, but I'll leave the door open."

Jake and Rosie jumped into bed, but by the light from the hall they could see right away that a funny little figure was crawling out from under Jake's bed. It was Fred. He seemed to be made of odd socks, including one of the ones with pompoms that Rosie had been given for Christmas.

"Has she gone?" he asked in a muffled voice. Sock monsters always talk like that.

"Yes, she has," whispered Rosie. "But if you're looking for socks again, you can't have any. We're fed up with finding only odd socks to wear."

"But I'm hungry," said the sock monster. "Isn't there anything else? I could manage a glove or a pair of mittens."

"We *need* those," said Jake. "We needed those socks, too."

"If I don't have something soon," said the sock monster, "I'm going to start munching your teddy bears."

"No!" cried Rosie. Now the twins knew that the sock monster was not a very nice monster, as monsters go.

"I know what to do!" whispered Jake. "You give him my scarf to nibble. I'll grab him!"

"Fnnnnffnnnfn!" shouted the sock monster, as Jake ran out of the room and down the stairs. There was no one about as he threw the sock monster into the washing machine and slammed the door.

Next morning, their mother put on a load of laundry. Later, when the twins saw it flapping on the line, they felt sure that the sock monster was gone for ever. Hmmm. What do you think?

# The Magic Quilt

Once upon a time, there was a woman who loved to sew. She made beautiful dresses for her daughters and handsome suits for her sons. They were made of the richest, brightest fabrics she could afford. Long after the children had gone to bed, she would sit by the light of a single candle and sew into the night. In the morning, she would be up earlier than anyone else, ready to go out to work for her family.

But the years passed. One by one, her daughters got married and left home. Of course, their mother sewed every stitch of their wedding gowns. Her sons went off into the world to seek their fortunes. They settled in faraway lands. From time to time, they sent letters home to their mother, but in all her busy life, she had never learned to read. She kept the letters in a chest, tied up with ribbons, until a friend from the nearby town could come to tell her what they said.

As the woman grew older, she could no longer work. She still loved to sew, but she could not afford the costly fabrics she had used before. At last, she became too weak to look after herself. Her friend invited her to stay. All she took with her was the chest from the foot of her bed.

Too frail to walk, the old woman lay in bed each day, watching the patterns made by the sun as it moved around the walls.

"If only you could read," said her friend, "it would give you something to occupy your mind."

That night, the woman dreamed of a special book with pages of red and blue and gold, full of stories and memories. The book was magic. If you touched it, the book could carry you to countries far away. In her dream, the old woman flew around the world, visiting her sons and daughters and bouncing her grandchildren on her knee.

Next morning, the woman suddenly knew what she must do. She asked her friend to open up her old chest and put it within her reach. Inside, as well as the letters from her children, there were all the scraps of fabric left over from her sewing over the years. Very carefully, she cut them into rectangles, like the pages of a book. Slowly, with stiff fingers, she sewed them together, until she had used all the pieces.

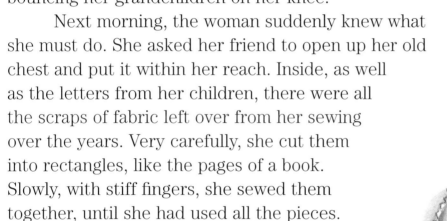

The beautiful quilt covered the old woman's bed from top to toe. As she smoothed her fingers over the fabric, in her mind she journeyed to far off places, thinking of the memories held by each piece of fabric.

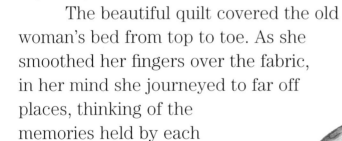

"This is a book that I *can* read," she said, and she never felt unhappy again.

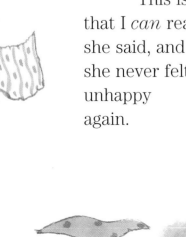

# A Bear With No Name

<W>hen a bear has found a good home, with children who love him, there is only one more thing he needs: a name. Having a name is what makes a bear feel he is no longer just one of hundreds of other bears, sitting on a toy shop shelf. A name gives a bear distinction. It helps him to know who he is. It is, in other words, Very Important.

And that is why, when the bear in this story had been in his new home for over a month and *still* hadn't been given a name, he began to feel very concerned.

"It's not difficult to think of a name," he muttered to himself. "I could be William, or Rufus, or Benjamin. Yes, Benjamin Bear is a good name. I don't know what's the matter with this family. You'd think they could have thought of something by now."

As a matter of fact, it wasn't very strange at all that the bear hadn't been given a name, for the little boy he now belonged to was only ten days old! The little boy could sleep, and he could cry, and he could drink his milk, but he couldn't do much else at all. He certainly couldn't *talk*. But the bear didn't understand about babies. He thought humans were like bears—able to walk and talk as soon as they were made.

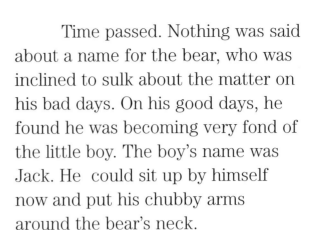

Time passed. Nothing was said about a name for the bear, who was inclined to sulk about the matter on his bad days. On his good days, he found he was becoming very fond of the little boy. The boy's name was Jack. He could sit up by himself now and put his chubby arms around the bear's neck.

"When he can talk," said the bear to himself, "Jack will give me a name. I know he will."

But things did not turn out as the bear expected. One morning, the little boy sat up in his bed and stretched out his arms. "Bear!" he said. "Bear! Bear!" It was his very first word.

"It won't be long now," said the bear. But although Jack was soon finding words for everything else in the house (even making up his own words for some things) he only ever called the bear "Bear!"

Then, one day, Jack had a new baby sister. Her aunt gave her a bear of her own, and from the very beginning everyone called the new bear Honey.

"And what is your name?" Honey asked Jack's bear, when he introduced himself.

The bear mumbled, but he couldn't avoid answering.

"He calls me Bear," he said, waiting for Honey to laugh.

But Honey didn't laugh.

"Oh, you are lucky," she said. "What a distinguished name. Only the very finest bear could possibly be called Bear!"

That night, when Jack snuggled down in his bed with his bear, he whispered, "Goodnight, Bear!" as he always did. And Bear could hardly sleep because he was almost bursting with pride.

"Goodnight, Boy!" he whispered back.

# Oh No, Not Again!

There was once a little elf who lived in a tree trunk. His mother and his granny lived there too. The elf's name was Juniper Jingle, and everyone liked him.

But Juniper's mother and granny found him very hard to live with. The daytimes were fine. It was nighttime when the problems started. You see, Juniper had wonderful dreams. Every night he dreamed he was flying over the mountains, or riding a unicorn, or dancing among the stars. They were lovely, magical dreams but they always had the same result. Juniper tossed and turned so much in his sleep that he fell out of bed.

You may not think that falling out of bed is such a bad thing, especially if there are soft cushions on the floor. But then you probably don't live in a tree. When Juniper fell with a thud, the whole tree shook. Mrs. Jingle woke up. Old Mrs. Jingle woke up. The squirrel who lived in the branches woke up. The rabbits who lived in the roots woke up (and there were a lot of them!) And the little bird who was building a nest at the very top of the tree had to start all over again. No one was happy except Juniper Jingle, who slept on as if nothing had happened … on the floor.

Mrs. Jingle had tried everything to keep Juniper in his bed. She put up rails … but he climbed them in his sleep. She tucked him in tight … but he threw off his covers without waking up. It was hopeless. Finally, she decided she must go to see the Fidget Fairy for a magic spell.

The Fidget Fairy was outspoken and not very polite. "It's his bed that's the problem," she said firmly.

"I can assure you it's the finest, most comfortable bed in the whole wood," protested Mrs. Jingle.

"But it's a bed for an ordinary elf," said the fairy, "and Juniper is a most extraordinary elf. An imagination like that should be encouraged. I will give you a spell to make him an imaginary bed, and everything will be well."

Mrs. Jingle was not convinced, but when she got home she said the spell exactly as she had been taught it. Juniper's old bed disappeared … and nothing came in its place. Mrs. Jingle was just about to go back to the fairy to complain when Juniper walked in.

"Wow!" he said. "Wow and double wow! That's a *wonderful* bed!" And he climbed up into mid-air and lay there, as comfortable as could be.

Juniper still has wonderful dreams, but no matter how much he tosses and turns, he never hits the floor. Mrs. Jingle is happy. Old Mrs. Jingle is happy. The squirrel and the rabbits are happy. And the little bird at the top of the tree now has the finest nest in the wood filled with babies of her own.

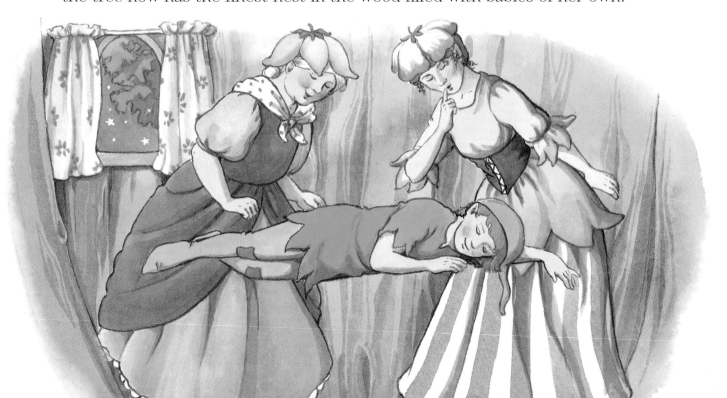

# Aunt Aggie Comes to Stay

The very first time Aunt Aggie came to stay with Louisa and her family, no one was prepared. They didn't guess that Aunt Aggie would arrive in a *truck*, or that she would bring *so much* with her! This is what she brought:

a huge trunk with exciting labels on it…

one pink, one orange, one yellow, one blue, and one brown case…

a picnic hamper that was extraordinarily heavy…

a guitar in a case with flowers painted all over it…

a striped bicycle with little flags on the handlebars…

several large bags with very strange things peeking out…

a parrot in a cage…

and…

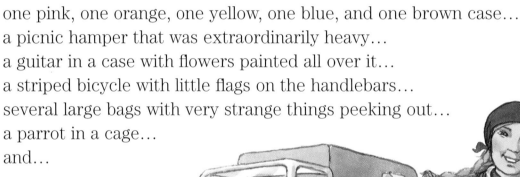

the biggest bunch of flowers you have *ever* seen!

By the time Aunt Aggie had moved everything in, Louisa's house felt very full. But Louisa didn't mind at all—there were such interesting things to see. Aunt Aggie seemed to have been *everywhere*, and she had wonderful stories to tell. Louisa *loved* having her to stay.

At last the day came when it was time for Aunt Aggie to go home. Into the truck went a huge trunk, one pink, one orange, one yellow, one blue, and one brown case, a picnic hamper, a guitar in a case, a striped bicycle, several large bags, a parrot in a cage, a huge box that had once contained a dishwasher, and Aunt Aggie.

"Goodbye!" she called, as she reversed dangerously into the road. "See you next year!"

It wasn't until ten minutes later that someone said, "Where's Louisa?" and someone else said, "*What* was in that dishwasher box?"

An anxious five minutes passed, and Aunt Aggie's truck came squealing up to the door.

"I can see," laughed Aunt Aggie, "you've been thinking what I've been thinking!"

That evening, when Louisa was safely tucked up in bed, and Aunt Aggie was far away, the little girl said, "Will she come back next year?"

"I'm afraid so," said Louisa's dad.

"Of course she will," said Louisa's mother.

"And will it be just the same?" asked Louisa.

"Yes," said Louisa's dad, "except we'll be checking *everything* in the truck before she drives away."

"Oh," said Louisa, and she fell fast asleep. After all, she thought, she had a whole year to think of a new plan.

# The Babyish Bear

When Jack was given a big present for his birthday, he was impressed. It was from Mrs. Marino, an elderly lady who lived nearby. Jack had never paid much attention to her before. He thought she was slightly strange, because she wore funny clothes and talked to herself as she walked down the street. But a present was a present, so maybe old Mrs. Marino had hidden depths.

As soon as he had ripped off the paper, Jack changed his mind. It was a bear! A great big fluffy teddy bear with a ribbon around his neck. Even Jack's mother hid a smile.

"How lovely, sweetheart," she said. "You must say thank you to Mrs. Marino when you see her."

Jack's mind was already on other problems. The bear had to be hidden—and fast. His friends were coming to his party in a couple of hours, and there was no way they could see this bear. If only it wasn't so enormous…

He tried to hide it in cupboards.
He tried to push it under the bed.
He tried to stuff it into the bag where the dirty laundry was kept.

Nothing worked. The bear was *there*. It was too big to hide.

Jack tried placing it in various positions around the house. Maybe it could just blend with the furniture somewhere? But he found that whenever he went back into the room, kind of pretending he didn't know there was a bear in there, the first thing to catch his eye was that silly, fluffy face!

It was almost time for the party when Jack had a brilliant idea.

"If I hurry, I've just got time to go and thank Mrs. Marino," he told his mother. She was suspicious, of course, but she let him go.

Jack struggled down the street with the bear. When Mrs. Marino opened the door, his words came out in a rush. "Mrs.-Marino-thank-you-very-much-for-my-present-but-it's-my-party-and-I'm-afraid-he-might-get-damaged-so-could-you-keep-him-for-me-this-afternoon-please?"

Mrs. Marino looked puzzled. "Well, you won't want a bear at your age, will you? Did you like the watch?"

Jack shook his head. What watch?

Then Mrs. Marino showed him the little opening in the bear's back where you could tuck things away. And she gave him the amazing watch that was inside and explained that she thought the bear would stop it getting squashed or stood on among all his presents.

"I was right," Jack told his mother when he got home. "She *is* strange, but she's okay too. More than okay. Oh look, it's *time* for my party!"

# Rainbow Ribbons

When an elf goes courting, he always takes the lady of his choice some ribbons for her hair. Elf girls are proud of their hair, which is thick and shiny. It also helps to hide their ears, which, as you know, are large and pointed. (Now there is nothing wrong with large, pointed ears, but some elf girls have been taking too much notice of the fairies, whose ears are so tiny you can hardly see them.)

Elderflower Elf went shopping one day for ribbons to take to Emmeline. He stood for some time in the shop full of ribbons and laces of every kind. It was hard to decide which ribbons to buy. In the end, he chose green ones, to match dear Emmeline's eyes. Then he wandered home in a haze of happiness, thinking about meeting her later, and fell into a ditch as a result, annoying a frog who lived there.

Unfortunately, Emmeline's beautiful eyes lit up for only a moment when she saw the ribbons.

"I was hoping you would bring orange ones," Emmeline sighed. "Elderflower? Elderflower?"

But the young elf was already gone, running back to the shop as fast as he could. Naturally, he didn't look where he was going, so he had another close encounter with the frog who lived in the ditch.

Emmeline considered the new orange ribbons for a second—before expressing a preference for blue.

Back went Elderflower. *Splash!* You guessed it. The frog was *not* happy. He wasn't happy ten minutes later, either, when Elderflower dashed by with red ribbons and landed right on his nose.

Back at her rose bower, Emmeline saw Elderflower approaching once more, clutching bunches of red ribbons. She sighed. Somehow there was something about Elderflower that just didn't appeal to her, especially when he was panting so hard he couldn't talk. She was just about to send him off for violet ribbons, just to get rid of him, when…

"I wonder if these are to your taste, my dear?" said a deep voice, and a jumping gentleman in green offered her a bow of beautiful rainbow ribbons.

Well, Emmeline married her frog and lived happily ever after. And Elderflower? He realized how well ribbons sell and is doing very well for himself in his own little shop in an oak tree!

# A Puppet For Polly

For her fourth birthday, Polly asked for a puppet. She didn't ask nicely. She didn't say "please". She said, "I want a puppet!" very, very loudly. That was the kind of little girl Polly Chin was.

Polly's dad was firm. She couldn't have everything she wanted, he said. But Polly's Aunt Naomi just smiled. On the little girl's birthday morning, there was a package from Aunt Naomi and inside was a big, beautiful, clown puppet. Polly ignored all her other presents and started playing with it at once. She found she could make the puppet do anything she liked, and she loved it.

"Time for swimming!" called her dad a little later. "Get your things, sweetheart."

"No!" said Polly. "Come with me, Mr. Clown. We'll hide in my bedroom."

"No!" said the puppet.

Polly was so surprised, she dropped him!

"Ow!" cried Mr. Clown. "I wish I hadn't come here, if that's how I'm going to be treated."

"I'm sorry," said the little girl, which was not something she often said. She picked up Mr. Clown and carried him to her room. She was going to hide under the bed and play with him

when her dad had given up trying to make her come out, but somehow she didn't like the knowing look the puppet was giving her… Polly collected her swimming things and left.

That night, after swimming, and a special lunch, and her birthday party, and lots more presents, Polly played with her puppet again. But Dad was already calling up the stairs.

"Time for bed, birthday girl!"

"Not yet!" shouted Polly.

"No way!" said the puppet. Once again, Polly looked in disbelief.

"I mean," Mr. Clown went on, "we haven't finished playing yet, and I won't be sleepy for hours. That man is rude and mean."

Now those were the kinds of things that I'm afraid Polly had very often said to her father, but she felt angry to hear someone else saying them.

"He's *not* rude and mean!" she said. "And I'm ready for bed. In you go!" She pushed the puppet into her toybox and shut the lid.

"Quite right," said Mr. Clown, much to Polly's surprise.

It didn't take Polly long to realize that when *she* was naughty, *Mr. Clown* was naughty too. And when she was good… well, you can imagine. Her dad noticed the difference.

"You know," he told his older sister Naomi, "ever since she's had that clown, she's been a nicer child. What a relief!"

Naomi smiled. "I remember" she said, "how it worked with a naughty little boy *I* grew up with."

But Polly's dad, like Polly sometimes, pretended not to hear.

# Why Am I Blue?

Once upon a time, there was a little blue elephant. Little Blue lived with his family on a dusty plain, munching and marching, marching and munching. When he wasn't munching *or* marching, what he loved best was rolling in the mud of a waterhole.

One day, the elephants came to a waterhole that was not as muddy as usual. It had clear, clean water, sparkling in the sunshine.

"No unseemly haste, please!" said Great-Grandmother Elephant, who could see that some of the younger members of her family were about to break into a trot. They swayed their trunks to show that they understood and moved forward at a sedate pace toward the pool. Mother Elephant ushered Little Blue to the front. She didn't want him to be left behind.

Little Blue reached the waterhole and looked down. Another little elephant looked back at him.

It was the first time that Little Blue had seen his reflection. It was wonderful! He swung his trunk one way. So did the other elephant. He swung it the other way. The other elephant did the same. Then he delicately put his trunk into the water and kissed his reflection.

It was only when he was full of the clear, clean water that the little elephant turned to his mother and asked, "Why am I blue?" Little Blue could see now that none of the other elephants looked at all like him.

"You are blue because blue is right for *you*," Little Blue's mother replied. "Some elephants are pink, some are blue, some are yellow, and some are like me, sort of dusty."

But Little Blue wasn't sure. He had never seen another blue elephant. He felt strange and different.

Then, one day, far away across the plain, he saw a wonderful sight. Pink, yellow and, yes, *blue* elephants were strolling along just ahead. Without a second thought, Little Blue scampered to meet them.

The new elephants were very friendly. Little Blue felt so happy to see other grown-up elephants who looked just like him. "I shall stay with these elephants," he said.

But that night, as he tried to sleep under the stars, Little Blue realized he didn't really belong with the strange elephants. His own mother was sleeping faraway across the plain, and maybe she was missing her blue baby. All by himself, under the huge moon, he trotted back to his own family.

"I'm so glad you're back, Little Blue," whispered his mother, sleepily.

"Mother, I like being blue," he whispered back. "Blue is just right."

"And you are just right, too," said his mother. "Now go to sleep, Little Blue. *All* elephants need their rest, even blue ones."

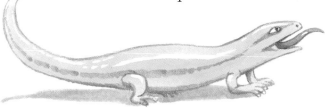

# Are You There, Mr. Bear?

All day long, strange noises came from Mr. Bear's house. There was clattering and banging and, I'm sorry to say, some angry words, too. It went on for hours, and everyone wondered what Mr. Bear could possibly be doing. It sounded as though he was moving furniture around, but no one was brave enough to knock on the door to find out. Mr. Bear had always been short tempered. Just recently, he had been more sharp and snappy than usual.

"Maybe he's spring cleaning," said Ragged Rabbit.

"Don't be ridiculous," replied his wife. "It's August."

By the end of the afternoon, a small crowd had gathered outside Mr. Bear's house. Still the strange noises went on.

"He wouldn't hear even if we did knock and offer to help," said a panda, which made everyone feel much better.

As the moon rose in the sky, the animals wandered back to their own homes. Gradually the noises from Mr. Bear's house stopped. There was complete silence for half an hour. Then the gentle sound of Mr. Bear's snoring could be heard, like a big cat purring.

The next morning, Ragged Rabbit happened to be passing just as Mr. Bear came out of his front door.

"Morning, Rabbit!" he beamed. "And a wonderful morning it is, too!"

"M-m-m-morning," stammered Ragged Rabbit. It was a very long time since he had heard Mr. Bear say anything cheerful. He watched in amazement as Mr. Bear strolled off down the street, greeting everyone he met with a friendly word and a wave.

When Ragged Rabbit told his wife about it at lunchtime, she put down her spoon at once. "It's not natural," she said, "and I'm going to find out what's happened. I'm going to see Mr. Bear."

Much to her husband's surprise, she was back in five minutes.

"I met Mr. Bear in the lane," she said, "and soon found out all about it. He's been bad tempered because he hasn't been getting a wink of sleep.

Some birds built their nest under the eaves and kept him awake with their twittering. All day yesterday he was hauling his big brass bed downstairs, where he can sleep in peace. He was cheerful because he'd just had his first full night's sleep in weeks."

"So it's safe to visit him again?" asked Ragged Rabbit.

"Not for long," replied Mrs. Rabbit darkly. "A family of mice has just moved in under the sitting room floorboards. Their scampering is worse than twittering any day."

# All at Sea

Petunia Panda was reading a bedtime book to her little ones. It was a rhyme about an owl and a pussy-cat who sailed away in a beautiful pea-green boat. All the baby pandas loved it, especially Patrick. His mind was so full of sailing and bong-trees and piggywigs that he began to dream about them as soon as his head touched the pillow. But Patrick's dream started to go wrong from the very beginning.

Patrick's boat wasn't pea-green. It was red. And he wasn't sailing away with a pussy-cat sitting quietly in the boat. Oh no. He was sailing with a kangaroo!

"Please don't bounce!" cried Patrick. "Please don't bounce!"

"Of course not," said the kangaroo. But kangaroos are so used to bouncing, they don't always know when they are doing it. The kangaroo in Patrick's red boat was good for a very long time … until Patrick saw an island on the horizon.

"Look!" he shouted.

"Where?" cried the kangaroo. And she bounced in excitement.

The next moment, Patrick found himself in the wettest water he had ever known. It was much wetter than water in a bathtub, and it was moving about! As the waves splashed into his ears, Patrick looked around for the kangaroo.

"Come up here!" she called. The upturned boat was floating nearby, and the clever kangaroo was sitting right on top of it. She dragged Patrick out of the water so that he could dry in the warm sun.

Slowly the upturned boat drifted toward the island. Patrick held on tight to the kangaroo, who had an extraordinarily good sense of balance. (It must have been all that bouncing.)

At last the boat landed with a bump on the sandy shore of the island. Patrick wondered what would happen next.

"I think we're meant to dance by the light of the moon," said the kangaroo, almost as if she had read Patrick's thoughts.

"But it's daytime," said Patrick, looking up at the palm trees. And just as he did so, a coconut tumbled down and bounced off his head.

"Ouch!" To Patrick's amazement, he wasn't asleep any longer, but his little brother Peter was banging him on the head with his toy kangaroo.

"I've been awake for ages," announced Peter. "I'm glad you've woken up at last."

"So am I," said Patrick, rubbing his head. "So am I."

# The Rainy Day

**M**rs. Millie Mouse looked out of the window. at the rain "Poor, poor Daphne!" she sighed. "Today of all days!"

Mr. Mouse knew exactly what she meant, but he was busy reading his newspaper and didn't want to be drawn into a conversation about The Wedding. He had heard about nothing else for months. Mrs. Mouse's sister Daphne was getting married. She was not a young mouse, but running her gardening business had left her little time for going to the dinners and parties where most mice meet their partners. Then, one day, she had visited a busy carpenter mouse to order a fence. The rest was history.

Mrs. Mouse put on her raincoat and hat and hurried out into the rain. She needed to visit her friends to discuss the dreadful calamity. They had to decide what to do with the mountains of food they had all been preparing. More important still, what were they to do with the extraordinary and amazingly huge hats they had all made, each trying to outdo the other?

Mrs. Mouse found all her friends at Mrs. Martha Mouse's house, which was the biggest in the wood.

"I'd love to offer to have the wedding here," cried Mrs. Martha Mouse, "but there simply isn't room for three hundred guests. I wish we could postpone the wedding, but what about all the food? My cook has been working hard all week!"

"Underground, maybe?" queried Millie Mouse. But one of the others cried out at once.

"Oh no! It would be so dark and cramped. And my hat won't fit any of the passages!"

"Besides," said Martha Mouse, "I refuse to have anything to do with those rabbits after what happened to my rock garden." (Martha Mouse's rock garden had become a large hole overnight, when a young rabbit with little sense of direction decided to pop up and look at the moon.)

Now you may notice that we have not yet met Daphne and her fiancé Tom. As a matter of fact, neither of them wanted all this fuss, which had been arranged entirely by the mouse ladies without stopping to ask if it was wanted at all.

While the ladies chattered, and the rain poured down, the two mice who should have been more worried than anyone were smiling happily. Their dream of a quiet wedding had come true after all as they stood beneath a young oak tree with only the Reverend Alfred Mouse for company.

"I love the rain," whispered Daphne, "don't you?"

"Almost as much," whispered Tom, "as I love you."

# Trouble in the Toy Box

When Leila went to bed at the end of a long and exciting day, she fell asleep almost at once. It was her birthday. In the morning, there had been presents and a special breakfast. Then her dad had taken her to the swimming pool and she had whizzed down the water chute seven times, which was more than she had ever whizzed before. After lunch, Leila's friends came to her party, and there were more presents. Just after the friends went home, Leila's granny visited and there were even more presents. And that is why the trouble began.

While Leila slept peacefully in her bed, there was a terrible groaning and sighing from her toy box. It was a special box, shaped like a pirate's chest, that her uncle had given her *last* year for her birthday.

"That panda is sitting on my elbow!" said a grumpy voice.

"You'd feel worse if you had a train standing on your toes," moaned another voice.

"That's no fun," cried the train. "I hate it when my wheels are wiggly."

"We were fine in here," said the ragdoll firmly, "until all these new toys arrived today. They should go."

"Did you see how happy Leila was when she opened us?" asked a yo-yo. "If anyone has to go, it's the old toys."

"I can't stand this any more," said the old panda, who was very worn and fragile. "I've got to get out of here!" He pushed and wriggled until he could open the lid of the chest and tumble out onto the floor. Lots of the other toys followed him, and the train, who was sometimes pretty clumsy, knocked the lid shut as he jumped out.

"Now we're stuck," said the ragdoll.

"I don't care," the panda replied. "It's better out here."

Next morning, Leila's dad shook his head when he saw all the toys over the floor, but he soon realized it would be hard to squeeze them all back into the toy box.

Just then, Leila's uncle arrived. "I'm sorry I couldn't make it yesterday," he said, "but I've brought your present today."

"Oh no!" Leila's dad groaned. "We've got enough trouble finding room for the presents we've got already."

But Leila's uncle just grinned. "Then it's a good thing I couldn't think of a different present this year," he said. And he carried in … another enormous toy box!

That night there was no grumbling and groaning among the toys. They slept just as quietly as Leila.

# What's That?

One night, Baby Bear woke up to find the moon shining right through the window onto his bed. Suddenly, Baby Bear felt wide awake. And what's more, he felt hungry! He rubbed his tummy and tried to think sleepy thoughts, but it was no good. He knew that downstairs in the kitchen there was some apple pie. His tummy *needed* that pie. Pushing back his quilt, Baby Bear scrambled out of bed.

In his bedroom, the moonlight made it easy to see where he was going. But outside in the hallway, it was very dark. Baby Bear peered through the blackness. Putting the light on might wake Mamma Bear, who was, as Baby Bear knew only too well, an extraordinarily light sleeper. In any case, he was too small to reach the light switch.

Baby Bear set off along the carpet, feeling in front of him with his paws at every step. When he couldn't feel anything at all in front of him, he knew he had reached the stairs. Although it was still just as dark, at least he could hold onto the stair rail now.

"Not far to that pie now," said Baby Bear to himself. But just then, he heard a noise.

"What's that?" he worried.

There was silence. After a few moments, Baby Bear went on down to the bottom of the stairs.

But as he turned toward the kitchen, he heard another sound.

"What's that?" he wondered.

There was silence again. Cautiously, Baby Bear put his hand on the kitchen doorknob. He opened the door rapidly to get the squeaking over as quickly as possible and…

"What's that?" cried a deep voice.

"What's that?" squeaked Baby Bear.

As the kitchen light was flipped on, he found himself face to tummy with Papa Bear … and Papa Bear was holding a large slice of apple pie!

The two bears looked at each other for a long minute.

"If I gave you a little bit of pie," said Papa Bear, "you won't need to wake Mamma Bear, will you?"

"If I don't wake Mamma Bear," said Baby Bear, "you won't wake Mamma Bear, will you?"

"It's a deal," said Papa Bear. "We must munch very quietly."

And so they did.

# Birthday Books

Grown-up people can be very bad at remembering things. They forget keys and hats and anniversaries almost every day. So how is it they (usually) remember your birthday? That's the work of the birthday fairy, who whispers in their ears a week or so before each important day.

The fairies have a special book, where all the birthdays in the world are written down (even grown-up ones). Long, long ago, there was just one Birthday Book. Nowadays, there are hundreds and hundreds of them, all kept in the Lilac Library. A very old elf has been the librarian for years and years. He is helped by a team of lively little elves, who are very good at running up and down the ladders that reach up to the highest shelves.

One day, there was a terrible commotion in the Lilac Library. A book had gone missing! It was the one for October 17th, Volume 96.

"It must have been misplaced," said the Chief Librarian, when an anxious fairy reported the problem. "Elves! Go and search every shelf to find the missing volume!"

The elves searched all day. Then they lit little lamps and searched all night. But they could not find the missing book.

The fairy concerned was beside herself with anxiety. "I must start reminding parents today," she said. "It's already the 10th of October."

"Don't worry, my dear," cried the Chief Librarian. "This has never happened before and it won't happen now, if I have anything to do with it. Come back in half an hour and I'll have a list of names for you."

As soon as the fairy had gone, the old elf pressed a secret button under his desk. A whole shelf of books swung open, and the Chief Librarian slipped inside to his secret room. It wasn't full of spells and potions. It wasn't full of cobwebs and cauldrons. It had a neat little desk and a computer with a big smile on its screen.

"Can I help you, Librarian?" it asked.

The old elf's fingers flew over the keyboard. In no time at all, the computer whirred and whizzed. The printer clicked and hummed. And a long list of all the birthdays for October 17th curled out of the machine.

When the Chief Librarian emerged from his room, the fairy was delighted with the list, although the elf swore her to secrecy about his back-up system. "It doesn't go with the elf image somehow," he explained.

And when the Chief Librarian got back to his desk, he found he had been sitting on the missing volume all the time. (You see, elves are often a lot like grown-ups, too.)

# The Tumbling Clown

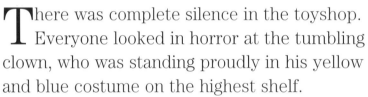

There was complete silence in the toyshop. Everyone looked in horror at the tumbling clown, who was standing proudly in his yellow and blue costume on the highest shelf.

"Don't be ridiculous!" cried the fluffy panda. "All your stuffing will fall out!"

"I can't bear to look!" whispered the little blue rabbit.

"If you're silly enough to do it, I can't stop you," said the jumping frog. "But even I wouldn't attempt a leap like that."

The tumbling clown put his nose in the air. "None of you has any idea of my abilities," he said grandly. "I was made to tumble and tumble I will! Can I have a long drumroll, please, Pink Teddy Bear?"

"Don't do it, Teddy!" yelled the panda, but that bear's only real skill was playing the drum and he went right ahead.

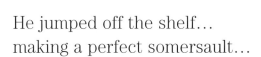

*Drrr! Drrr! Drrr! Drrr!*
The tumbling clown raised his hands in the air.

He jumped off the shelf…
making a perfect somersault…

and a double back flip…..
He touched his toes…..

and landed on his feet on the back of one of the elephants belonging to the toy Noah's ark.

"There'll be no stopping him now," muttered the panda.

"Is it over?" asked the little blue rabbit.

"Wow! That was great!" cried the jumping frog. "Will you show me how you did it?"

"Of course," said the tumbling clown.

So the next day, the jumping frog performed an even more amazing acrobatic display than usual. The day after that (much to his own surprise) the panda tried a small somersault himself. And by the end of the week, even the little blue rabbit could do a double-eared spin with tail twist.

So, if you have a little brother or sister whose toys are always flying out of the bed or buggy, you'll know it's not the baby's fault at all. Those toys have been taught by the tumbling clown, and they won't stay still no matter what you do!

# A Bear at Bathtime

Johanna wanted to take her bear everywhere. She took him to playgroup. She took him to visit her friends. She took him to the park. And, of course, she took him to bed with her. The only problem with Johanna and her bear was bathtime. Every night there was a battle.

"Sweetheart, he *can't* go in the bathtub," Johanna's mother would say. "He'll get soaking and soggy. You won't be able to take him to bed with you and I'm pretty sure his paws would shrink."

But Johanna didn't want to listen. She was sure that her bear was just as alive as any of her friends. He listened to everything she said. And her friends didn't get soggy in the bathtub! Johanna looked carefully at her hands and feet. They certainly didn't shrink in the water. Johanna decided her mother was wrong.

But mothers can be very determined. Each night at bathtime there were loud words from Johanna, and there were firm words from her mother. There was not very much at all from her teddy bear, who was forced to sit on a shelf until Johanna was dry and ready for bed.

I suppose it had to happen one day…. Johanna's Aunt May came to babysit one evening. Aunt May knew, of course, that bears don't go in bathtubs, but she didn't know she had to watch Johanna every *second* of bathtime. In went the bear, hidden by the bubbles. It wasn't until Johanna dragged the soaking, furry toy out of the bathtub that Aunt May saw what happened. She was horrified.

"You can't take a wet bear to bed with you, and that's final," she told the little girl. Well, there were loud words from Johanna, and there were firm words from her aunt. There was plenty of dripping from the teddy bear.

Aunts can be very determined, too. When Johanna went to sleep at last, Aunt May took the bear down to the drier and popped him in. Much later, she tucked him into bed beside Johanna.

Next morning, Johanna's mother looked curiously at Johanna and her bear as they sat down for breakfast.

"Your bear looks smaller," she said with a frown.

Secretly, Johanna thought so, too. But she couldn't say that to her mother. Johannas can be determined, too.

"He isn't smaller," she said. "It's just that *I've* grown."

# No More Cake!

When Agatha Mouse hopped on the scales in the bathroom one morning, she let out a little shriek of alarm. All the little mice, who were cleaning their teeth after breakfast, jumped.

"Oh no," groaned Ethel. "It's no-more-cake-time."

"It certainly is," sighed their mother. "I'm afraid it's no-more-cake-for-a-long-time."

The little mice sighed, too. They knew what their mother was like during no-more-cake times. She was miserable. She was grumpy. She had to shut her eyes when they walked past all the bakeries in town (and often bumped into other mice as a result). But worst of all, she stopped baking. She didn't make pies. She didn't make cookies. She didn't make puddings. And, of course, she didn't make cakes! Agatha Mouse was well known as the *best* cook in the area. When she stopped baking, it wasn't just a blow to the little mice. They found that several of their friends stopped calling, and interest in their school lunchboxes suddenly disappeared.

But there was no stopping Agatha when she made up her mind. She decided she needed more exercise, too, so she walked to school to collect the little mice instead of zooming along in her little red car. The little ones didn't mind having to walk home, but it made them late for the latest episode of *The Masked Mouse* on television each day. As they trooped home, no one would have guessed that they really were a very happy mouse family.

Agatha Mouse's no-more-cake times could sometimes last for weeks. The little mice gritted their teeth and tried not to think about muffins and pies. You can imagine how surprised they were when, only a couple of days later, they came home from a game of hide-the-acorn to find Mrs. Mouse baking and singing in the kitchen.

"So it's not no-more-cake-time any more?" asked Ethel.

"No," smiled Agatha. "It's no-more-being-naughty-little-mice-time. It's finding-your-mother's-slippers-for-her-time. It's can-we-do-anything-to-help-you-dear-mother-time."

The little mice looked at each other. What *was* she talking about?

Agatha Mouse gave them all a big hug and an acorn muffin.

"My dears," she said, "you are big little mice now, and that's how you must behave. We're going to have some babies! That's why the scales said I was heavier. Now get ready for bed. And make the most of it! Very soon it's going to be waking-up-in-the-middle-of-the-night-time!"

# The Sniffles

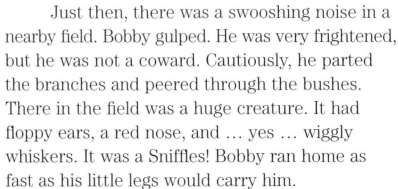

Bobby Bunny was getting ready to go out to play when his mother called him back.

"You need your scarf on a day like this," she said. "We don't want you catching the sniffles, do we?"

Bobby was puzzled. "How do Sniffles look?" he asked.

"Droopy ears, a red nose, and wiggly whiskers," said his father from behind his newspaper.

Bobby ran out to join his friends. He had a wonderful time. When at last he realized he must hurry home, the sun was already beginning to go down.

The trees made dark shadows on the lane as Bobby scuttled along. It grew darker. Bobby was a brave little bunny, but he suddenly began to think about the Sniffles. More than once he turned his head to make sure there wasn't a Sniffles creeping along behind him.

Just then, there was a swooshing noise in a nearby field. Bobby gulped. He was very frightened, but he was not a coward. Cautiously, he parted the branches and peered through the bushes. There in the field was a huge creature. It had floppy ears, a red nose, and … yes … wiggly whiskers. It was a Sniffles! Bobby ran home as fast as his little legs would carry him.

"Bobby!" cried his mother. "We're so glad you're home. But whatever is the matter?"

"It's the Sniffles!" cried Bobby. "I saw it in a field. It had floppy ears and a red shiny nose. And its whiskers were wiggly."

Father Bunny looked puzzled for a moment. Then he grinned. "That sounds like the Sniffles all right," he said. "Let's go and see if we can find it, son. We can't have a Sniffles around here."

So Bobby Bunny and his father walked quietly down the lane. When they reached the right place, Bobby pulled at his father's coat and pointed.

Very carefully, Father Bunny parted the bushes. Then he shone his powerful flashlight right onto the face of … a scarecrow!

Suddenly, Bobby felt a whole lot better.

On the way home, his father explained what the sniffles really were.

"I've learned something very important tonight," announced Bobby with a smile. "It's not catching the sniffles you have to worry about, it's the sniffles catching *you*!"

# The Balloon Bear

When a cross little girl called Emily went to the fair with her grandma, she was very hard to please. Grandma bravely went on all the rides, but Emily said they were boring. Grandma bought Emily sweets and treats, but the little girl still didn't smile. Then Emily spotted a man selling balloons of every size and shape. "I want one of those," she said.

Grandma was tired and wanted her granddaughter to be happy, so she let Emily choose a balloon shaped like a bear. Emily didn't say thank you when the string was put into her hand. She just marched off toward the gates and home, with Grandma behind her.

Maybe it was because Emily was in such a hurry that a lady coming the other way bumped into her. It was only a little bump, but Emily let go of her balloon. The bear went floating up into the air and was out of reach before Emily even noticed it was gone.

"Buy me another one!" demanded the little girl. Grandma looked for the balloon man, but he had disappeared.

"I want to go home," said Emily. "I've had a horrible time."

Grandma was a very patient woman, but she was beginning to feel almost as cross as Emily.

What Emily and her grandma didn't notice as they walked home was that the balloon bear was bobbing along above them. He was still there when they reached Emily's gate and saw her mother cutting flowers.

"How was the fair?" she asked.

"Boring," said Emily.

"And the rides?"

"Boring."

"You must have had a very boring afternoon," said Emily's mother to her grandma with a sympathetic smile. At that moment, the balloon bear floated gently down, down, down, onto the roses. *POP!* it went—just behind Emily, who sat down with a bump and a surprised expression on her face.

"Well, there *was* one bit I did enjoy," said Grandma with a grin.

And all three, including Emily, laughed together at last.

# One by One

Mr. Noah studied his charts. "I've built it exactly as I was told," he said to his wife, "but still, it doesn't look right somehow."

"The ark is fine," said Mrs. Noah. "It's just the door that looks out of proportion. Are you sure you got the measurements right?"

"I've checked and checked," replied her husband. "It's high time we started loading the animals. I don't like the look of those clouds."

Ham, Shem and Japhet began to organize the animals. "Two by two, please," they called, nudging the gnus and shooing the sheep.

Dutifully, the animals lined up. And although there was a little pushing and shoving from the hippos, and the jaguars were taking a suspiciously friendly interest in the rabbits in front of them, it was all pretty orderly.

"Let the loading begin!" cried Mr. Noah grandly. Two by two, up the plank, trotted the flamingos and the porcupines. Two by two came the butterflies and the peacocks. Two by two came those difficult hippos…

Ooops! Oh dear! There was no doubt about it, two hippos side by side would *not* fit through the door.

"I knew it!" cried Mr. Noah. "I'm afraid you'll just have to go in one by one. It doesn't sound quite right, I know, but as long as two of every creature are on board, it can't really matter."

One by one went the zebras. One by one went the rhinos and the kangaroos. One by one went the elephants… Ooops! Oh dear! There just was no way that even one elephant would fit through the door.

"That settles it!" said Mr. Noah. "Those elephants are meant to be on board. Although I'm sure I've done everything I was told, I simply must have made a mistake. Come on, Ham, we've got work to do!" Mr. Noah set to work there and then to make a much larger doorway with two fine doors.

After that, there was no trouble loading the animals, and as the clouds gathered overhead, Mr. Noah consulted his lists for the last time.

"I'm missing one tiny flea!" he called. "Mrs. Flea, come along please!"

As he spoke, a tiny speck hopped off his chart and jumped into the ark.

Mr. Noah peered at the paper. "Bless my soul, what a difference a zero makes," he said. "No wonder I got the measurements wrong. Now let's hope there's room on that ark for *me*!"

# Clip, Clip, Clop

Dusty the horse leaned over the gate. "What are you doing, Percy?" he asked.

"Ssssh!" said Percy Pig. "Don't interrupt me, old friend. I'm reading my book."

Dusty blew through his nose rudely. "Poo!" he snorted. "I don't know why you want to do that. Come and play Chase with me instead."

"You don't like reading because you're not very good at it, Dusty," said Percy. "And that's because you don't do it enough. You need some practice, that's all. Then you could read just as well as I can—and you'd like it a lot more."

Dusty kicked up his heels and snorted again. "It still seems boring to me," he said, "and books are always about silly things anyway."

"Well, that's where you're wrong, old friend," replied Percy. "This book happens to be about a horse, and it's very interesting."

Dusty looked dubious. He tried to peer over Percy's shoulder, but Percy turned away.

"I really can't read with you blowing in my ear," he complained. "Let me finish this story and then I'll come for a trot down the road with you."

Dusty was not in a very good mood by the time Percy joined him. He was sulking and sighing as the two of them set off. In fact, he deliberately trotted off at a faster pace than Percy's little legs could go.

"Just a minute, Dusty," puffed Percy, "there's something I need to talk to you about."

"Well?" said Dusty shortly.

"It's just that in my book," said Percy, ignoring the snort this brought from his friend, "the horse went *clip, clop, clip, clop* down the lane. But I couldn't help noticing that you're going *clip, clip, clop, clop, clip, clip, clop, clop*."

Dusty looked down at his hooves. One of his shoes was very loose and he'd been sulking too much to notice.

A quick trip to the blacksmith soon fixed Dusty's problem. "It's a good thing you got it fixed so quickly," said the blacksmith. "You could have hurt yourself."

Nowadays, Dusty has a new respect for books. So if you happen to see a horse and a pig reading together in a field, you'll know who they are, won't you?

# Be Brave, Lian!

Lian was afraid of dragons. Although everyone told her not to be silly, she lived in a country where the storybooks were *full* of dragons. It was true that no one had seen one for years, but Lian just knew that the first one to turn up in a long time would head straight for her. She never went anywhere without a big silk bag containing her secret anti-dragon kit. I don't know what was in it, but even Lian didn't put all her faith in it. Her real plan, when the dreadful day arrived, was to run.

Months passed, and Lian had almost began to stop worrying, when she set off one day for her grandma's house, which was over the hill and through the woods. The hill was very steep, but Lian was fit from all the running practice she did every day. She soon reached the top and set off down the other side. It was then that it happened.

Far below among the trees, there was a great big puff of smoke. And then another one. And then another one. Lian knew at once it wasn't a woodman's fire. It was moving! It was moving more quickly than anything she had ever seen.

There was absolutely no doubt in Lian's mind. There was an enormous dragon down there.

But even as she turned to run, Lian had another thought. Her grandma was down there, too. And she couldn't run very fast at all. Lian was frightened of dragons, but she loved her grandma very much. Without thinking about it too hard, she set off down the hill toward the smoke, clutching her anti-dragon kit.

The smoke had stopped moving now, but the dragon was making a dreadful noise, roaring and panting down in the valley. Lian ran faster. When she reached her grandma's house, she rushed in without knocking.

"Ah, here you are!" said Grandma. "Isn't this exciting?"

Exciting? Being eaten alive? Exciting? But Grandma had grabbed Lian's hand and was dragging her out of the house.

The panting and roaring got louder as Grandma hurried along, and when Lian looked up, she found that the dragon's smokey breath was all around.

"There it is!" cried Grandma. "The very latest way to travel. It's called a train. Hurry! It's about to leave!"

Years later, Lian told her own children about the dragon that was a train. They smiled at her silliness and shook their heads. But then, they didn't know *their* children would one day ride in a dragon that could fly, did they?

# Don't Look Behind You!

Fred Rabbit was tired of taking his cousin Nibbles to school. Nibbles was a whining, frightened young rabbit, who imagined foxes behind every bush and owls on every gate post. The trouble was that with such a vivid imagination, he never noticed when there really was something dangerous ahead. Fred had pulled him out of ditches and disentangled him from fences more times than he cared to remember. One evening, on the way home from school, he decided to teach Nibbles a lesson.

Just as the two young rabbits were passing the spooky oak tree at the corner of the lane, Fred paused dramatically and hissed, "Don't look behind you, Nibbles!"

"W-w-why not?" stuttered Nibbles.

"Because I'm pretty sure we're being followed by a Hoojymop," said Fred, "and you don't want to meet a Hoojymop on a Monday."

"W-w-why not?" asked Nibbles, trembling to his toes.

"Because although Hoojymops are cuddly, friendly creatures all the rest of the week," whispered Nibbles, "on Monday nights, they have to eat rabbit pie. It's the Hoojymop law."

Nibbles was so frightened he could hardly walk. "W-w-w-what can we do?" he stammered. "I d-d-don't want to be a p-p-pie!"

"Just keep walking," said Fred, "and keep looking ahead. If we're lucky, we'll see a fox or an owl."

"L-l-l-lucky?" gasped Nibbles. "Why would we want to see one of them?"

"Because they love to eat Hoojymops," explained Fred, "better than they love to eat bunnies. Keep a sharp lookout!"

But although both little bunnies peered into the gloom, they didn't see a fox or an owl, and they reached home safely.

It wasn't until they were washing their paws before supper that Nibbles suddenly let out a piercing squeak. "It's Tuesday!" he yelled. "Fred, that Hoojymop wouldn't have eaten us after all."

"Nothing will eat us if you use your head , Nibbles," said Fred, "like you're using it now. If you think about what frightens you, you can make it go away. Even a Hoojymop."

# Doctor Do-A-Lot

When Doctor Do-A-Lot came calling, it was like a hurricane blowing through the house. He zoomed in through the front door, rushed upstairs to the patient, hummed and haahed, and dashed back down again before you could say, "Good morning, Doctor, fine weather we're having." In fact, before you said "Good…" he thrust a piece of paper into your hand and whirled down the front path, waving his top hat.

The piece of paper was one of Doctor Do-A-Lot's famous prescriptions. Some of them were the kind of thing you would expect.

Others were a little stranger.

Everyone in Elftown loved Doctor Do-A-Lot, so you can imagine how upset they were when they heard that the doctor himself was not feeling well. Several elves went to visit him and found him lying in bed, looking pale and ill. But when they asked if he had toothache, or tummy ache, or fidgety feet, he said no. He didn't, he said, have anything that could be found in his medical books. He was as puzzled as anyone else about what was wrong with him.

The elves were worried. They were worried about Doctor Do-A-Lot and they were worried about themselves. What would happen when they needed the doctor? Everywhere you went in Elftown there were elves whispering together on street corners. Because they were whispering, it was some time before Old Mrs. Mapleleaf heard about the problem, for her ears were not as sharp as they had once been. But when she was told what had happened, she let out a cackle and began to scribble on a piece of paper.

"Take this to Doctor Do-A-Lot," she said. "He'll soon get better."

And when the doctor saw the paper, he burst into laughter and shooed everyone out of his house.

"I need to get some rest," he said. "I'll see you all next week."

And the paper? Doctor Do-A-Lot framed it and put it on his wall. It said:

_Doctor Do-Too-Much's medicine_

_Take twelve hours of rest every day, mixed with proper meals and a dash of common sense._

_Mrs. Mapleleaf_

# Little Cousin Clare

When Bryn heard that his little cousin Clare was coming to visit, he was very excited. He lived on a farm, a long way from the nearest village, and he didn't have any brothers or sisters. Straight away, he began to plan the games he would play with Clare.

Bryn got out all his trucks and cars and arranged them in a line. He decided Clare could choose first which to play with, although he couldn't help hoping it wouldn't be the big blue one. Next he organized all his painting things. He piled stacks of bright paper on the table and lined up his paints and brushes.

"I'm glad to see you're tidying up, Bryn," said Dad, when he came in from the fields. "Your playroom looks much better now."

But Bryn hadn't finished. He started to sort out his books and put all the ones about animals and all the ones about trucks together. He wondered for a moment if Clare would like different kinds of books, as she was a girl, but he couldn't imagine anyone not liking animals and trucks. After all, his mother was always driving the big tractors on the farm.

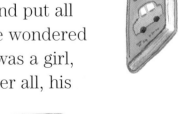

Last of all, Bryn made a big effort to organize his building bricks. It took ages because he had lots of them. Finally, he was ready.

Bryn was too excited to eat much breakfast the next day. He was waiting for the sound of wheels in the driveway. They came, of course, the moment he wasn't looking out of the window. When he heard his mother flinging open the door and shouting above the noise of the car, Bryn ran up behind her and tried to peep around her legs for his first sight of Clare. All he could see was a lady carrying something wrapped up in a blanket.

"Bryn," smiled his mother, "I want to introduce you to your Aunt Jo."

Aunt Jo bent down. "And I want to introduce you to your little cousin Clare," she said.

Bryn looked right into the face of a tiny, sleeping baby.

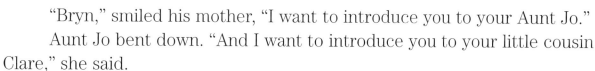

"Um… Excuse me," he said. "I just have to put some things away."

"He's been very tidy recently," his mother told Aunt Jo. "He's growing up so fast."

As Bryn put away his trucks, his painting things, his books and his bricks, he didn't really feel bad that Clare couldn't play with them. It meant he had a little more time to have the big blue truck all to himself. He would lend her his big blue bear instead. After all, there's nothing like a baby to make you feel much more grown-up than you've ever been before.

# A Christmas Concert

As Christmas drew nearer, the little mice who lived among the roots of the oak tree became more and more excited. Every evening, they twirled together red and orange leaves to make garlands. They drew their own Christmas cards and counted out their tiny mouse money to make sure they had enough to buy presents for friends and families. On the Friday before Christmas, Mrs. Mouse was taking them shopping at the edge of the forest. They couldn't wait.

But two weeks before Christmas, it began to snow. The big white flakes floated down thick and fast. The little mice jumped up and down with excitement. It was going to be a white Christmas, and there would be sledging and skating and snowballs!

All week it snowed. On Thursday evening, Mrs. Mouse called the little mice to her and spoke seriously.

"I'm sorry, my dears," she said, "but the snow through the forest is so thick, we won't be able to visit the shops tomorrow."

The little mice looked at each other. What about the presents they had planned to buy?

"You are clever little mice," said Mrs. Mouse. "I'm sure you could make your own presents if you tried hard."

The little mice worked hard for the next few days, and they were surprisingly good at making presents. They made little acorn bowls and paper planes. They threaded seeds to make necklaces and painted pretty pictures. By Christmas Eve, all the presents were made, except one.

"What are we going to make for Great Aunt Mouse?" they asked.

The trouble with great aunts and grandmothers and other wise old mice is that they already have everything they need. They have more acorn bowls and necklaces and pictures than you can imagine.

"Well, think about what she likes," suggested Mrs. Mouse.

"She likes music," said one little mouse.

"She likes little mice," said another.

"We could put on a special Christmas Concert for her!" said a third.

And that is exactly what they did. While the snow drifted down outside, the little mice sang carols, played their drums and whistles, and danced a special Christmas dance. It was a huge success. Every year since, the little mice have entertained all the grown-up mice as far as the edge of the forest and back (if it's not snowing too hard).

# I Can't Fall Down!

The monkeys were chattering in the trees and bright sunlight was splashing the glossy leaves of the forest. Mrs. Parrot took her youngest son out on a branch and told him what he had to do.

"Just uncurl your feet and let go, Percy," she said. "And then flap your wings as hard as you can."

Percy peered through the leaves. "Mamma," he said, "I can't fall down!"

"It's not a question of falling down, Percy," said his mother sharply. "It's a question of flying. Your sisters can do it. Your brothers can do it. Every single one of your relatives can do it—except your little cousins and they're still in their eggs. Now, don't be a baby. Just let go."

But Percy was not convinced. "Monkeys don't fly," he said. "Snakes don't fly. Even elephants don't fly."

"And thank goodness for that!" cried Mrs. Parrot. "No, Percy, none of those animals, poor things, can fly. But parrots can! You can! Go on!"

Percy lifted one foot. Then he lifted the other foot (but he put the other one down first).

"That's just shuffling," said Mrs. Parrot. "It's not swooping, or twirling, or flying. Come on, Percy. I've got lots to do this morning."

But Percy simply wouldn't let go. When his mother gave him an encouraging nudge, he clung on tightly with his little feet. He wobbled. He wibbled. But he didn't let go. Mrs. Parrot sighed and left him to it.

"You were quite right," said a voice near Percy's ear. It was a young monkey, swinging from a nearby branch. "It's much better being a monkey and not flying," said the new friend. "Just follow me!" And the monkey strolled off along the branch.

Percy followed hot on his heels. It was fine! No flying at all! Even when the monkey speeded up a bit, Percy still hopped along confidently. And when the monkey said, "Now, here you have to jump," Percy simply didn't think about it. He jumped.

Oh! Before he knew what was happening, Percy had given a little flap of his wings and was swooping through the leaves. He tried a twirl. He tried a dive. He tried a double somersault with spin and back flip. It was wonderful! He was flying.

Mrs. Parrot watched proudly from a nearby branch. "Thanks, Mavis," she said to a young monkey who was passing.

"Anytime," laughed Mavis.

# By the Light of the Moon

Faraway on the top of the world, there is a place that is always cold. As far as you can see, there is only white snow and the icy sea. There are no trees and no flowers at all. There are only seals and fish and bears. Yes, there are big white, furry bears. And when those polar bears are about, the seals and the fish need to watch out, because those bears can creep ever so quietly…

and slide ever so slippily…

and run ever so quickly…

and dive down into the deep blue sea with hardly a splash, when they are looking for a snack.

"I love being a polar bear!" one little bear told his mother once. "There is so much space for creeping and sliding and running and swimming, and the sun shines all the time and makes the snow sparkle."

"Well, that is true in a way," said his mother, "but you are only a little bear and have not yet been alive for a whole year. In the summer the sun shines all the time, even at night. But in the winter, the sun doesn't shine at all. Not in the daytime and not in the nighttime."

The little bear went away to a cosy ice cave to think. And the more he thought, the more he felt very, very sad. The long, dark winter was coming. How could he creep and slide and run? How could he dive and swim and swish after those shiny little fish if he couldn't see where he was going? He was worried and frightened, and after that day, although he played and swooshed as often as before, he was sometimes sad.

It wasn't very long before the sun began to go away for part of the day. At first, the little bear didn't notice, because he was asleep. Then, one night, he woke up and everything around him was deep blue and velvety.

"What has happened?" he asked his mother.

"The sun has gone away until next year," she replied. "It is winter now."

The little bear looked around. It wasn't frightening and it wasn't worrying. He could still creep and slide and run and dive, but now instead of sparkling, the snow was shining with a silvery light.

The little bear looked up. "The sun hasn't gone," he said. "Look!"

But his mother shook her head. "That is the moon," she said, "and the moon will keep us company all through the winter, until the sun comes again."

The little bear gave a huge sigh. There wasn't anything to worry about. In the daytime and the nighttime, in the summer and the winter, he still lived in a wonderful world.

# Ting-a-ling

Ting-a-ling was an elf with a problem. He had a little blue hat with a bell on the end of it. Yes, that is how he got his name. Everywhere he went, the bell on the hat went *ting-a-ling! ting-a-ling!* Of course, there's nothing wrong with having a bell on your hat. There's nothing wrong with going *ting-a-ling! ting-a-ling!* all the time. But this little elf had a special job to do, and the bell made this terribly difficult.

You see, Ting-a-ling was an artist and his special job was painting the wings of butterflies. He was brilliant! He could paint the most beautiful rainbow patterns that shimmered and shone. The difficulty was that butterflies can be very nervous creatures. You may have seen them flitting about, never stopping still for long. The only way to paint them is to wait until they are sitting on a leaf and having a little snooze in the sun. Then you must work as lightly and quickly as possible before they wake up.

I'm sure I don't need to tell you what Ting-a-ling's problem was. His butterflies always woke up too soon. He would lean back to take a look at his work and the bell on his hat would jingle. In a flash, the butterfly would flap her wings (spoiling the pattern, if they were still wet) and fly away. It was a disaster.

Ting-a-ling didn't know what to do. He was able to keep his head still for a pretty long time as he painted, but he couldn't do it for ever. He couldn't bear to see half-painted butterflies flitting around the garden. The other elves were beginning to complain. And he couldn't take his

hat off either, because it was held on by magic. He didn't give up, but he became more and more unhappy.

One morning, Ting-a-ling started work on a butterfly sitting right on the edge of a leaf. He could only reach one wing, but he hoped the butterfly would move a little bit in her sleep. He had managed to finish one whole wing when, forgetting about his hat, he put his head on one side to admire his work.

*Ting-a-ling! Ting-a-ling!* The butterfly flapped her wings together and flew off at once—with a beautiful pattern on both wings! When she pressed her wings together, the wet paint on one wing had made a pattern on the other wing that was just the same!

After that, Ting-a-ling was a very happy elf. He always painted just one wing, yet all the butterflies looked beautiful. And his little bell was never a problem again.

# It's Too Quiet!

Mrs. Bear sat having coffee with her friend Mrs. Katt. Their children were playing in the next room, so the two ladies had a moment for a chat and a cookie. But all of a sudden, Mrs. Bear looked up. An expression of concern crossed her face.

"Are you thinking what I'm thinking?" she asked her friend.

"I am," said Mrs. Bear in ominous tones. "It's too quiet in there."

Mrs. Katt and Mrs. Bear hurried to the door. The next room was deserted—but the window was wide open!

"Oh, my paws and petticoats!" cried Mrs. Bear. "Where have those naughty young cubs gone?"

"When I catch those kittens…" muttered Mrs. Katt darkly.

Mrs. Bear and Mrs. Katt tramped across the countryside, looking for their little ones. It was not a difficult trail to follow, for those kittens and cubs had left all kinds of things along the way. There was a bonnet on a bush and a toy under a toadstool. And there were little pawprints everywhere.

By the time Mrs. Bear and Mrs. Katt caught up with the runaways, they were hot and muddy and hungry. As you probably know, mothers who are hot and muddy and hungry are not very happy. The cubs and kittens only had to look at the cross faces peering at them across the clearing to know that they must pack up their picnic, which had seemed *such* a good idea, and hurry home.

That evening, Mrs. Bear was still cross when Mr. Bear came home from the forest. When he heard what had happened, he gave the cubs another lecture and looked sympathetically at his wife.

"Tomorrow, Karl Katt and I will look after the children," he said, "so that you and Karen Katt can have a day off. Those little ones really are a pawful these days."

Mrs. Bear agreed with enthusiasm. The next morning, she sat with her friend once again, enjoying her coffee. But in the back of her mind, she felt that something was wrong. She frowned.

"Are you thinking what I'm thinking?" she asked Mrs. Rabbit.

"I'm afraid so," replied her friend. "I hate to say it, but I'll be so glad when those little ones come home."

"So will I," agreed Mrs. Katt.

Both ladies laughed together.
"It's just too quiet everywhere!"

# The Perfect Present

Perhaps you have heard of Ellie Elf, who knows more magic than any elf in the seven kingdoms. Long ago, her grandmother taught her an important lesson. It was Ellie's birthday, and she had lots of presents, but she found it hard to enjoy them because she kept wondering what her grandmother would bring her. The old lady's presents were always special and often had something magical about them.

It was late in the afternoon when Ellie's grandmother arrived, wearing her old-fashioned bonnet and shawl. When the old lady was sitting comfortably and sipping a cup of bramble tea, Ellie went to stand by her side. Grandmother smiled.

"Of course," she said, "it's a special day today, isn't it? And I have something here for you, little one. Hold out your hand."

Ellie did as she was told. She could hardly keep still, she was so very excited.

But when she looked down at her hand, all there was in it was a little pile of dusty seeds, some so tiny she could hardly see them.

"Plant them in the garden and see what happens," said her grandmother.

Ellie was disappointed. Perhaps she hadn't understood. "Are they magic?" she asked.

The old elf-lady looked at her curiously. "All seeds are magic," she said. "Wait and see."

Ellie did plant her seeds. And she waited. And waited. And waited. For the longest time, nothing happened at all. When some little green shoots finally appeared, they were not very exciting. Ellie lost interest in her seeds and didn't go near the corner of the garden where she had planted them for weeks.

Then, one morning, her grandmother came to visit again. "I've come to see your seeds," she said with a smile.

Ellie felt guilty. She was very much afraid the plants would be brown and dead. But when she led her grandmother to the furthest corner of the garden, she cried out with pleasure. There were flowers everywhere!

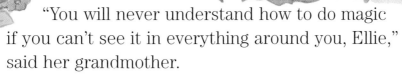

"You will never understand how to do magic if you can't see it in everything around you, Ellie," said her grandmother.

Today, Ellie Elf is as wise as her grandmother once was. "The world is so magical," she says, "it hardly needs any help from me. At least, only a little bit…!"

# The New Toys

Late one night, Daniel Harris's new toys decided to leave home. It wasn't really because Daniel didn't play with them very much. That wasn't his fault. He had been in bed with a very bad cold ever since his birthday. But while Daniel had been getting better, the toys had passed the time by looking at his books. The new toys had never seen books before. The pictures of mountains and lakes and sailing ships were so exciting. They were amazed to find that somewhere in the world there were castles and dragons and monsters.

"There is so much to see in the world, we can't just stay here," said the deep-sea diving doll. "I want to visit the real sea."

"I agree," said the yellow digger. "There are whole mountains for me to dig, but all I can do is run up and down the carpet!"

"And I'd like to run on some real rails," said the little red engine. "These ones only go as far as the window."

So that night, the toys crept out of the bedroom door and made their way down the stairs. It was hard work for the digger and the engine, but the diving doll helped them as much as he could.

The toys soon found the back door of the house, but it was shut. Luckily, it had another little door in it, used by the cat, so by piling up some cans and boxes, the toys managed to squeeze through and set off down the path. The moon was shining bright and clear to light their way.

But those toys hadn't gone far before they stopped.

"The world is much, much bigger than I thought," said the diving doll.

"I know what you mean," agreed the digger. "I could dig these flower beds for ever and ever and I still wouldn't finish."

"And I'm beginning to think my little wheels wouldn't fit on great big tracks," sighed the engine. "It's not how I thought it would be at all."

The toys talked a little longer and decided to return home. The big wide world was just too big and too wide.

Next morning, Daniel was feeling much better and could begin playing with his new toys. After a long and happy day, his mother read him a story in bed before he went to sleep.

The toys listened and smiled knowingly.

"You know, there are a lot of things in books," said the diving doll, "that are just made up. I didn't believe that story at all."

"Neither did I," said the digger.

"I certainly didn't," said the engine.

And, you know, that was very strange, because the story was … this one!

# The Wind Who Went Away

Once upon a time, there was a fierce and fearsome wind who blew all day long around the little village of Belton. He lifted the laundry from the washing lines and blew it over the hedges. He crept under the tiles on the roofs of the barns and sent them tumbling to the ground. He even scurried around the skirts of the ladies doing their shopping and made their petticoats blow up so you could see their stripey stockings! And the poor old rooster on the weather vane swung around and around and around until he was dizzy.

The good people of Belton got together to decide what to do.

"We could build another windmill to use up the wind," suggested one man, but the miller objected that his business would be halved.

"We could stay indoors," suggested an old lady who didn't get out much anyway.

"We could pay the wind to go away," said the bank manager. "Although I'm not sure what he would do with money."

In the end, no one could agree about what to do, so the meeting broke up and the people went home to their houses, blown and buffeted all the way.

Now, the wily old wind had been listening at the windows, pushing cold fingers in through the cracks and making the ladies pull their coats tighter around them. He decided he would teach the villagers a lesson. There and then, he packed his bags and went off to the mountains.

The next day, everything was still. For a few hours, everyone was very happy. Then the complaints began.

"I can't fly my kite!" cried the miller's son.

"My laundry won't get dry!" groaned the greengrocer.

"The sailing ship bringing my goods from China is stuck out in the bay," said a merchant. "There is no wind to bring it in to shore."

And the rooster on the weather vane grumbled even more. "I've been looking at the same view for hours now," he said. "I'd like a change of scene."

But the wind took his time over his visit to the mountains. He caused a few blizzards and avalanches and had a wonderful time. In fact, I think he is still there, puffing and blowing around the snowy peaks.

I wish I could say that the people of Belton are more careful now about complaining, but they're not. The other day, I heard them moaning that the summer was too hot. I'm very much afraid the sun heard them too.

73

# Look Out!

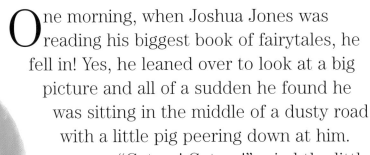

One morning, when Joshua Jones was reading his biggest book of fairytales, he fell in! Yes, he leaned over to look at a big picture and all of a sudden he found he was sitting in the middle of a dusty road with a little pig peering down at him.

"Get up! Get up!" cried the little pig. "The wicked old wolf is right behind us and we must get home to my house before he comes."

Joshua Jones was surprised to find himself in the picture. He was even more surprised to find a little pig talking to him, but he was still dazed from his fall, so he ran along after the pig.

But when Joshua saw the pig's little house, he stopped suddenly.

"Come on!" cried the pig. "We've no time to waste!"

Joshua Jones shook his head. "I've read this story," he said, "and your house is no good. It's made of straw and the wolf will huff and puff and blow it down."

"I think it's a beautiful house," said the little pig. "Are you sure about the huffing and puffing?"

"Absolutely sure," said Joshua Jones.

"Then we must run on up the road to my brother's house," said the little pig. And off they went.

But when Joshua saw the little pig's brother's house, he shook his head again.

"This house is made of sticks," he said. "The wolf will huff and puff and blow it down. Trust me."

The little pig found this hard to believe, but Joshua was firm.

Five minutes later, Joshua Jones, the little pig, and the little pig's brother were running down the road toward their last brother's house.

"We must hurry," said the little pigs. "The wolf can run very fast. Look, he's coming over the hill!"

When the little pigs reached their brother's house, they were very relieved that Joshua Jones nodded his approval of the little brick building. In two seconds, the door was shut and Joshua Jones and the three pigs were sitting inside—squashed, but safe.

And when the wicked wolf arrived, he was so breathless from running, he couldn't huff or puff at all! He dragged himself back home and ate some leftover apple pie instead.

What happened to Joshua Jones? Well, as there was no fire in the grate, he climbed right up the chimney and out of the book—just in time for his own supper.

# Clarissa Cow

Sometimes a chance remark can change your life forever. That is exactly what happened to Clarissa Cow. Before it happened, she was a very ordinary cow indeed, and she knew it. Afterwards—well, you'll see.

One day, George, who looked after the cows on White Fence Farm, brought his little niece to see them. He sat her on the gate and held on to her tightly as she looked across at the munching animals. Of course, one or two of them came across to say hello, as cows do, and one of these was Clarissa.

As soon as she saw the friendly cow, with the big white patch on her forehead, the little girl smiled. "Look!" she said, "it's the cow that jumped over the moon!" She was thinking of her book of nursery rhymes, in which there was a picture of a cow exactly like Clarissa and the whole rhyme about the cat, the fiddle, the cow, the moon, the little dog, the dish, and the spoon. I expect you know it.

But Clarissa the cow did not know it. She looked up at the little girl with interest and, for some reason, George's niece recited the whole poem, clapping her hands as she did so, Then George took her off to have some cookies in the farmhouse and left Clarissa with a head full of very silly ideas.

That very same day, Clarissa began jumping. She knew you could not see the moon until it was night, but she thought it would be a good idea to have a practice now. *Thud! Thump! Lump! Thud!* Clarissa was not an elegant cow. She did not jump with grace and skill. She jumped just as you would imagine a big, heavy cow with a tummy full of milk to jump.

The other cows hurried down to the opposite corner of the field. They felt sure something was badly wrong with Clarissa. Anyway, no one wanted to be in the way of one of Clarissa's landings!

That night, Clarissa waited until the moon was big and full. She jumped and she jumped and she jumped, but there was no way she could even touch the moon, never mind jumping over it. Clarissa felt sad as she walked slowly back to her barn.

But in the barnyard there was a puddle. And in the puddle … there was a moon! Clarissa couldn't believe it. She gave herself plenty of space for a run-up. She trotted as fast as she could … and she jumped—right over the moon!

Of course, no one saw it. And no one would have believed it if they had been told. But from that day to this, Clarissa has walked as proudly as a queen, and *everyone* can see that.

So you see, it's the things you feel on the inside that are important, because somehow everyone can see those too.

# The Precious Baby

Once upon a time there was a very precious baby. Everyone loved the baby. They tickled and the baby giggled. They said *coo, coo, coo* and the baby said *goo, goo, goo*. They rocked the baby and the baby smiled. They swung the baby and the baby laughed. They threw the baby up in the air and the baby cried *OOOOOOOH!* and came down safe and sound.

Each night the baby's chubby, waving arms and fat, kicking legs splished and splashed in the bath. The bubbles winked, and the little ducks bobbed, and the baby giggled and squiggled. Then with a one, two, three, a big fluffy towel went all the way around the baby's slippery little body. There was squeezing and cuddling and bouncing … and bed.

There were so many cuddly toys in the baby's bed, there was hardly any room for the baby. Every night, there was snuggling and kissing and someone who loved the baby very much said, "Goodnight, darling. Goodnight, honeybun. Goodnight, sweetheart. See you in the morning!" And the baby smiled and went to sleep … almost every night. And in the middle of the night, sometimes the baby felt a butterfly kiss, light as love, on baby hair.

78

When the baby was sniffly and snuffly, there was always someone close by. When the baby had new teeth coming through and was red and cross, someone who loved the baby very much said, "Shh, shh, shh. It's all right.. This will make you feel better." When the baby woke up in the night and wanted to play, someone said, "Oh no, not now. Please, not now. Go back to sleep, cherry plum. Everyone loves you. Shut your little eyes. There."

In the morning, the baby was the first one to wake up. The baby's bright little eyes looked all around. The baby's fat little feet bounced on the bed. The baby's little pink mouth opened wide and let everybody know it was time to get up. Then someone sleepy who loved the baby very much came along and said, "Come with me for just one cuddle. Then we'll get up. Just one cuddle. Just one." And the baby's eyes closed again for one half of a cuddle, then it was time to start the day.

And so it went on, and it seemed a very long time to the baby. But it was a nice time. And then one day the baby heard someone say, "Our baby isn't a baby any more. Our baby is growing up. How quickly the time has gone." And the baby wrapped chubby little arms (that weren't so chubby any more) around the someone's knees and kissed them.

Do you know who that baby was? That baby was you! Goodnight, darling. Goodnight, honeybun. Goodnight, sweetheart. See you in the morning!

# Index of Themes